BACK
to the
BASICS

Learning to Walk the Walk

Pastor Charles E. Young Sr.

Copyright © 2023 Pastor Charles E. Young Sr.

All rights reserved. No part of this book may be reproduced, stored, or transmitted by any means—whether auditory, graphic, mechanical, or electronic—without written permission of both publisher and author, except in the case of brief excerpts used in critical articles and reviews. Unauthorized reproduction of any part of this work is illegal and is punishable by law.

ISBN: 978-1-63950-217-2 (sc)
ISBN: 978-1-63950-218-9 (e)

This publication contains the opinions and ideas of its author. It is intended to provide helpful and informative material on the subjects addressed in the publication. The author and publisher specifically disclaim all responsibility for any liability, loss, or risk, personal or otherwise, which is incurred as a consequence, directly or indirectly, of the use and application of any of the contents of this book.

Writers Apex

Gateway Towards Success

8063 MADISON AVE #1252
Indianapolis, IN 46227
+13176596889
www.writersapex.com

www.cacbethel.com
www.igoeministry.com

CONTENTS

Acknowledgements v
Objective Aim vii
How to Use This Book ix

Part 1: Starting At Ground Zero

Lesson #1:   The Power, Cost, and Sacrificial Love of God 2
Lesson #2:   Subjective, Interpersonal & Redemptive Consequences 6
Lesson #3:   The Mercy of God 14
Lesson #4:   Transition From Sinners to Saints 18
Lesson #5:   Taken Under Siege 23
Lesson #6:   Changing Under Fire 27
Lesson #7:   The Valley of Decision 32
Lesson #8:   Which Way Have You Chosen? 38
Lesson #9:   Are You A sheep or A Goat? 44
Lesson #10: Understanding & Standing on God's Promises . 48
Lesson #11: Submission, Subjection, Endurance 53
Lesson #12: Follow Me 58
Lesson #13: Preparing for the Rain 62
Lesson #14: The Sign of a Reprobate Mind 67
Lesson #15: Are You Ready to Meet Jesus? 71
Lesson #16: Stepping into Trouble 80
Lesson #17: Subjective & Interpersonal Consequences 84
Lesson #18: Recovering From Family Crisis 86
Lesson #19: Understanding the Spiritual and Physical Effects of Sin 89

Part 2: How to Walk Close to the Heart of God

Introduction: First Things First 92
Lesson #1:   Diligence 100
Lesson #2:   Virtue 103
Lesson #3:   Knowledge 108
Lesson #4:   Temperance 112
Lesson #5:   Patience 114
Lesson #6:   Godliness 116
Lesson #7 & #8: Brotherly Kindness/Brotherly Love 118

Part 3: The Blessing, Loss and Restoration of Dominion

Lesson #1:   The Blessing of Dominion 124
Lesson #2:   The Loss of Dominion 127
Lesson #3:   The Restoration of Dominion 129

Part 4: From the Garden to the Cross

Introduction: Root Cause 134
Lesson #1:   Where It All Began 135
Lesson #2:   Grace Found in an Unexpected Place 139
Lesson #3:   Reviewing the Cross & Reevaluating
             Christianity 143

Final Words From the Author 156
About the Author 157

ACKNOWLEDGEMENTS

My first and foremost dedication is to my Lord and Savior Jesus Christ, who through suffering on the cross for my sins, has allowed me to preach the Gospel. I dedicate this to my children, family and friends.

I am grateful to all of the pastors and ministers who have allowed me to grace their pulpits, time would not permit me to thank you all individually.

I am grateful for my father who taught me to have a strong work ethic and to my mother who taught me compassion through her own suffering.

I also dedicate this work to my nine living siblings, whose characters have helped me learn how to deal adequately and compassionately with different kinds of personalities.

I will never forget where I came from and the Lord God who saved me.

OBJECTIVE AIM

The aim of this book is that it becomes a blessing to you as it has been to so many others. Each lesson is derived from life's experiences. For example, the lesson taken under siege was given at a time when everything that could go wrong in my life went wrong! I was just about ready to give up when the Lord revealed that I was taken under siege by my circumstances. I had been a robotics programmer for fifteen years and always had enough money for what I needed. In July of 2000, I was injured and could no longer work. My income went from $85,000 per year to $14,426 per year on disability. It was then that I realized that I no longer had control. It was then that I knew that my only place to refuge was and is in Jesus Christ my Lord. I understand that gain is not godliness, but obedience to the Word of God. The real blessing comes while we are changing under fire, it is a time when you, by faith will go against everything that you feel, and trust the Lord no matter what the consequences are.

HOW TO USE THIS BOOK

This book is more of a WORKbook than a reading book. It is my hope that by time you have finished this book, you will have built up a storehouse of scripture in your soul. The opening line of Charles Dickens', A Tale of Two Cities, "It was the best of time, it was the worst of times", so aptly fits the time in which we currently live. We enjoy all of the modern conveniences but we have not held onto the lessons and the disciplines of the past. This book will cause you to put some work in. It is my desire that you dive into the Word of God, pull up the scriptures and engage with them. Let the Word speak to you, have a conversation with the love letter that was written with you in mind.

As you go through the pages, you will notice many spaces available for note taking. Interact with the scriptures and allow the Holy Spirit to give you a revelation of what God is saying.

His grace truly is sufficient,

Pastor Charles E. Young Sr.

STARTING AT GROUND ZERO

LESSON #1

THE POWER, COST, AND SACRIFICIAL LOVE OF GOD

Text: John 3: 14-17
Key Verse: Vs.16

Love: A profoundly tender passionate affection for another person.

Profound: How deep

Lesson Scripture: Mark 12:28-31

Heart: The innermost or central part of anything.

Soul: The principle of life, feeling, though and action.

Mind: The part of us that reasons, thinks, feels, wills, perceives, and judges.

Strength: The inherent capacity to manifest energy to endure and resist.

Notes:
_____
_____
_____
_____
_____

Read the reference scriptures and share your understanding of the scripture in the space provided.

John14:15, 21, 23

John 15: 9-17

John 21:15-17

Romans 5:8

Romans 8:28

1 Corinthians 13:1-13

Ephesians 5:1-2

1 Thessalonians 4:9

2 Timothy 1:9

LESSON #2

SUBJECTIVE, INTERPERSONAL & REDEMPTIVE CONSEQUENCES

Text: Isaiah 53:1-12
Key Verse: Vs.4

Subjective Consequences (Isaiah 7:14; Matthew 1:18, 21)

Interpersonal Consequences
(Romans 6:23; John 3:16; Ephesians 2:8, 9)

The Redemptive Consequences of Jesus has 3 Elements

1. Hostage
2. Ransom
3. Redemption

Sin Brings Interpersonal Consequences

1. Between man and God
2. Between the man and his wife
3. Between man and animals
4. Between man and nature

In each case let's see if we can find the Subjective & Interpersonal Consequences.

1. **Noah (Genesis 9:20-25)**

2. Abraham (Genesis 20:1-7)

_____
_____
_____
_____
_____
_____
_____
_____
_____
_____
_____
_____

3. Moses (Numbers 20:8-12)

_____
_____
_____
_____
_____
_____
_____
_____
_____
_____
_____
_____
_____
_____

4. Israel's Request for a King (1 Samuel 8:11-12)

5. David (2 Samuel 12:7-14)

6. **Jonah (Jonah 1:1-3)**

Jesus as Hostage: One delivered over to another as security for some future act. **(Matthew 26:47-50)**

Jesus as a Ransom: Payment for the release of someone **(Luke 22:1-6)**

_____
_____
_____
_____
_____
_____
_____
_____
_____
_____

Jesus as Redeemer for Redemption: The losing of someone by the paying of a price.

The Cost: John 18:1-11

_____
_____
_____
_____
_____
_____
_____
_____
_____
_____

Trial: Mark 15:1-15

_____
_____
_____
_____
_____
_____
_____
_____
_____
_____
_____

Crucifixion: Luke 23:44-49

_____
_____
_____
_____
_____
_____
_____
_____
_____
_____
_____
_____
_____

Resurrection: John 20:1-9

Notes:

LESSON #3

THE MERCY OF GOD

Text: Exodus 34:1-7
Key Verse: Verse 7

Grace: The kindness by which God bestows favor and blessings

Mercy: Compassionate or kindly forbearance shown toward an offender, an enemy, compassion, pity.

Kindness: Grace, favor

Notes:
_____
_____
_____
_____
_____
_____
_____
_____
_____
_____
_____
_____

Read the reference scriptures and share your understanding of the scripture in the space provided.

Psalms 59:9, 10, 16, 17

Psalms 86:5, 13, 15, 16

Psalms 103:8, 11, 17

Psalms 123:1-4

_____
_____
_____
_____
_____
_____
_____

Luke 1:49, 50, 54

_____
_____
_____
_____
_____
_____
_____

Romans 9:14-18

_____
_____
_____
_____
_____
_____
_____

Romans 11:29-32

1 Timothy 1:2

2 Timothy 1:2, 16, 18

LESSON #4

TRANSITION FROM SINNERS TO SAINTS

Text: Romans 5:12, 18, 19, 21
Key Verse: Vs.19

Sinner: one who falls short, a rebellious wicked person, we all became sinners through the fall of Adam (vs.19)

Romans 3:23

Romans 6:23

Saints: Title given to the believers I Christ our Lord

Philippians 1:1

_____
_____
_____
_____
_____
_____

1 Corinthians 1:2

_____
_____
_____
_____
_____
_____

What is the difference between a sinner and a saint?

1. Sinners are born (Psalms 51:5)
2. Saints are made (John 1:12)

Ephesians 2:8-9 (Grace)

_____
_____
_____
_____
_____

Grace: A heart surgeon preparing the heart of sinners to receive Jesus Christ as their Lord and Savior. The kindness of God's blessings upon the ill-deserving: it grants sinners pardon of their offenses.

Grace does 5 things:

1. **Grace makes sinners willing to receive Christ**
2. **Grace gives us favor before God**
3. **Grace delivers the sinner from the wrath to come**
4. **Grace destroys all the stronghold of sin and Satan**
5. **Grace teaches us to love and trust Christ Jesus.**

Grace brings forgiveness of sins.

Forgiveness: God's eraser, erasing our sins forever through repentance.

Grace opens the door to conversion.

Conversion: The turning of a sinner to God. **(John 3:16)**

Notes:

_____
_____
_____
_____
_____
_____
_____

Read the reference scriptures and share your understanding of the scripture in the space provided.

Isaiah 7:14

_____
_____
_____
_____
_____
_____
_____

Matthew 1:23

_____
_____
_____
_____
_____
_____
_____

John 14: 1-11

_____
_____
_____
_____
_____
_____
_____

Romans 10:9-13

Acts 4:12-13

Philippians 2:5-11

LESSON #5

TAKEN UNDER SIEGE

Text: Matthew 11:10-12
Key Verse: Vs.12

Take: To Seize or capture

Under: Subject to the control of a person drug or force, in or into a subjection or submission.

Seize: To take advantage of promptly to seize an opportunity.

Psalms 91:1-4: There are 3 Things that we allow to remove us from The Secret Place.

1. People
2. Places
3. Things

Suffer: To permit, endure, undergo pain.

Violence: Rough or injuries physical force, action or treatment.

Force: To overpower or overcome.

Signs of Being Under Siege

1. Anything that has taken over your home
2. Any person who deals with you by physical force
3. If you are in a place that dictates to you what you can or can't do
4. Your friends/children
5. Your thinking
6. Your husband/wife
7. Your love of anything more than God

Read the reference scriptures and share your understanding of the scripture in the space provided.

Matthew 11:1-6, 12

_____
_____
_____
_____
_____
_____
_____
_____
_____
_____
_____
_____
_____
_____
_____
_____

Acts 7:54-60

Acts 24:1-7

2 Samuel 22:1-4

Ezekiel 12:19-20

Micah 6:5-8

Habakkuk 1:1-3

LESSON #6

CHANGING UNDER FIRE

Text: 1 Peter 1:1-7
Key Verse: vs.7

Change: To transform or convert
Convert: To turn

In the fire of your trials, you must remember 3 things Jesus said:

1. I will not leave thee
2. I will not forsake thee
3. I will not fail thee

You must know 4 things about God:

1. It is impossible for God to break His promise
2. The times of testing are to make us more like Jesus
3. The Lord wants to break the power of the Devil
4. He wants to move you so that in the place of hardship you can see His hand and praise Him for keeping you.

Thought for Today: When a person who prays receives a blessing from God today and murmurs tomorrow, what is he doing? He is replacing the Word of God with his feelings. **What is this kind of person called?** They are called being double minded.

Read the reference scriptures and share your understanding of the scripture in the space provided.

Genesis 22:1-12, 18

Isaiah 48:10

Job 23:8-12

Job 42:1-5

Psalms 66:10-14

Proverbs 17:3

Hebrews 4:12-15

James 1:1-8

LESSON #7

THE VALLEY OF DECISION

Text: Joel 3:11-14
Key Verse: Vs. 14

Note: When you see a person whose life is full of trouble and turmoil they are at the valley of decision. (Proverbs 14:25)

When sickness has brought you to the very edge of death you are at valley of decision. (John 10:10)

Every situation in your life will bring you to the valley of decision. (Isaiah 1:18)

Valley: Any place, period or situation that is filled with fear, gloom and disappear

Decision: The act or need for making up one's mind (Josh. 24:1415)

The valley of decision for the believer is to be molded into the image of our Lord and Savior, Jesus.

The Christ (Matthew 16:16; John 10:27: Matthew 16:24; 2 Peter 1:1-10)

_____
_____
_____
_____
_____

The valley of decision for the unbeliever is for his or her salvation. (Isaiah 64:6)

The decision for Salvation is based on receiving Jesus Christ as Lord and Savior.

_____
_____
_____
_____
_____
_____
_____
_____
_____

The Process

Read the reference scriptures and share your understanding of the scripture in the space provided.

Romans 5:12, 17-19

_____
_____
_____
_____
_____
_____
_____
_____
_____

Matthew 1:18-25

_____
_____
_____
_____
_____
_____
_____
_____
_____
_____
_____

Matthew 11:11-28

_____
_____
_____
_____
_____
_____
_____
_____
_____
_____
_____
_____
_____
_____

John 3:2, 16

_____
_____
_____
_____
_____
_____
_____
_____
_____
_____
_____
_____

John 14:1-10

_____
_____
_____
_____
_____
_____
_____
_____
_____
_____
_____
_____
_____
_____

Ephesians 2:8-9

_____
_____
_____
_____
_____
_____
_____
_____
_____
_____
_____

Roman 3:23

_____
_____
_____
_____
_____
_____
_____
_____
_____
_____
_____
_____
_____

Romans 6:23

Romans 10:1-10

LESSON #8

WHICH WAY HAVE YOU CHOSEN?

Text: Matthew 7:13-14
Key Verse: Vs.13

Way: A road or journey, manner of life

Roads: Have to do with a pathway of life **(Proverbs 14:11-12)**

Jericho, Damascus, Emmaus

1. **Jericho:** is the road that everyone is born on it symbolizes sin and destruction it is on this road where the enemy seek to take your life. **(John 51:5; Romans 3:23; Romans 6:23, John 10:10)**

    a. Life on Jericho (Luke 10:25-37)

b. **Items of destruction (Galatians 5:19-21)**

2. **Damascus:** is the road of decision where you will meet Jesus when the course of life has caused great difficulty and we begin to look for a different way. It is on Damascus Road where the opportunity for the new birth to take place. **(Acts 9:1-6** Paul's Conversion)

a. It is on Damascus Road where this scripture comes to life (John 3:16)
   i. The Whosoevers
      1. The Murderers
      2. Liars
      3. The Drunk
      4. The Drug User/Dealer
      5. The Thief
      6. The Prostitute
      7. The Fornicator
      8. The Adulterer (etc.)

   ii It is on Damascus that Jesus says these words:
      1. Matthew 11:28-30;16:24-26

      2. John 3:1-7, 16;10; 14:1-6

3. **Ephesians 2:8, 9**

4. **Romans 10:1-15**

3. **Emmaus:** Road is where you will meet Jesus and follow Him until his return. It is a road of everyday growth with a rewarding end. **(Luke 24: 13-31)**

a. Continuing on Emmaus
   i. Luke 9:22-24

   ii. John 8:31-32;10:1-5

   iii. Romans 12:1-2

iv. 2 Timothy 2:15

_____
_____
_____
_____
_____
_____

v. Hebrews 13:5,8

_____
_____
_____
_____
_____
_____

vi. 2 Peter 1:1-10

_____
_____
_____
_____
_____
_____
_____

vii. John 14:1-3

_____
_____
_____
_____
_____
_____
_____

LESSON #9

ARE YOU A SHEEP OR A GOAT?

Text: Matthew 25:31-40
Key Verse: Vs. 31-33

Sheep: Were ceremonially clean animals used as a sacrifice for the people of God. It was symbolic of Jesus as our sacrificial lamb.

Shepherds: Are keepers of the sheep

The shepherd would pick a sheep to lead the herd and would put a bell on him, the purpose of the bell was two-fold:

1. It was to locate a lost sheep,
2. Or it was used on the head sheep so when the other sheep heard the bell they would follow the lead sheep, because of the ringing of the bell.

Goat: An animal often associated with the sheep but his disposition or character of the goat was opposite the sheep therefore it was less chose for sacrifice.

The problem with the goat is, his answer to everything is always "But" displays a second consideration to be compared with the first.

Sheep- follow the Word of God without Question. Today the Lead sheep is the Pastor (Jeremiah 3:15; I Peter 5:1-4)

Sheep will follow, Goats will 'but'

Read the Reference scripture and share your understanding of the scripture in the space provided.

The ringing of the bell represents the World of God. Can you heart the bell?

1. First Bell: John 10:1-5; 23-30

___

2. Second Bell: Hebrews 13:17

___

3. Third Bell: Hebrews 10:22-32

4. Fourth Bell: 2 Peter 1:2-10

5. Fifth Bell: Hebrews 12:1-8

6. **Sixth Bell: John 15:1-12**

7. **Seventh Bell: Ephesians 5:21; 6:1-4**

LESSON #10

UNDERSTANDING & STANDING ON GOD'S PROMISES

Text: 2 Peter 1:1-4
Key Verse: Vs. 4

Promise: A declaration that something will or will not be done.

Declaration: Something that is announced, avowed or proclaimed.

Stand or Standing: To remain firm or steadfast as in a cause; to take up or maintain a position or attitude with respect to a person. In this case the persons are God our Father and Jesus Christ our Lord and Savior.

Promises with Conditions

1. Deuteronomy 28:1-8

___
___
___
___
___
___
___
___
___
___

2. **Psalms 1:1-3**

_____
_____
_____
_____
_____
_____
_____

3. **Psalms 50:15**

_____
_____
_____
_____
_____
_____
_____

4. **Proverbs 3:5-6**

_____
_____
_____
_____
_____
_____
_____

5. Malachi 3:10-12

6. Matthew 6:33

7. Luke 6:38

8. John 14:1-3

9. Acts 16:25-31

10. 2 Corinthians 6:14-18

11. 2 Corinthians 9:6-8

12. Philippians 4:19

13. 1 John 5:13

LESSON #11

SUBMISSION, SUBJECTION, ENDURANCE

Text: James 4:1-10
Key Verse: Vs. 7

Submission: An act or instance of submission; submissive conduct or attitude

Submit: Yield, be subject

Read the reference scriptures and share your understanding of the scripture in the space provided

1. Colossians 3:16-21

_____
_____
_____
_____
_____
_____

2. Ephesians 5:21

_____
_____
_____
_____
_____
_____

3. **Hebrews 13:16, 17**

_____
_____
_____
_____
_____
_____
_____

4. **1 Peter 2:10-15**

_____
_____
_____
_____
_____
_____
_____
_____

5. **1 Peter 5:5-7**

_____
_____
_____
_____
_____
_____
_____

Subjection: Under authority, to place under

1. **1 Timothy 2:8-15**

1 Timothy 3:1-4

1 Peter 3:1-10

Endure: To abide, to bear up under, suffering

Read the reference scripture and share your understanding of the scripture in the space provided.

2 Thessalonians 1:1-4

_____
_____
_____
_____
_____
_____

2 Timothy 2:1-3, 10

_____
_____
_____
_____
_____
_____

2 Timothy 4:1-4

_____
_____
_____
_____
_____
_____

Hebrews 12:1-7

James 1:12

James 5:10-11

1 Peter 2:19-21

LESSON #12

FOLLOW ME

Text: Matthew 4:18-20
Key Verse: Vs.19

Follow:

Bible Dictionary: To go after

Webster: To go or to com after, move behind in the same direction

Author: To use as a direct or indirect object

_____
_____
_____
_____
_____
_____
_____
_____
_____
_____
_____
_____

Read the reference scriptures and share your understanding of the scripture in the space provided.

Jeremiah 17:13-16

Hosea 6:1-3

Matthew 9:9-13

Mark 6:1-4

Luke 9:23-24

John 1:35-43

John 10:27-30

John 12:26

John 21:15-19

Acts 12:1-8

LESSON #13

PREPARING FOR THE RAIN

Text: Hosea 6:1-3
Key Verse: Vs.3

Rain: To offer, bestow, or give in great quantity; to rain favors upon a person or people.

Let it Rain:

Wisdom

Knowledge

Understanding

Peace

Joy

Temperance

Holiness

Read the reference scriptures and share your understanding of the scripture in the space provided.

Exodus 16:1-4

_____
_____
_____
_____
_____
_____
_____

Leviticus 26:1-4

_____
_____
_____
_____
_____
_____

Deuteronomy 11:13-32

_____
_____
_____
_____
_____
_____
_____

Deuteronomy 28:9-13

2 Chronicles 6:21-27

2 Chronicles 7:12-16

Isaiah 55:6-13

Joel 2:23-27, 32

Psalms 68:9

Zechariah 10:1

James 5:7, 8

Hebrews 6:7

LESSON #14

THE SIGN OF A REPROBATE MIND

Text: Romans 1:18-32
Key Verse: Vs. 28

Reprobate: That which is rejected on account of its own worthlessness. (Jeremiah 6:30, Hebrews 6:8) A castaway or rejected because they have failed to make use of opportunities offered them.

Reject: to put away

Castaway: One regarded as unworthy (! Corinthians 9:2&; Matthew 22:1-8)

Notes:

_____
_____
_____
_____
_____
_____
_____
_____
_____

Read the reference scriptures and share your understanding of the scripture in the space provided.

1 Samuel 15:18-28

Jeremiah 6:19, 27-30

Hosea 4:1-6

Zachariah 11:6

2 Timothy 3:1-8

Titus 1:10-16

Hebrews 6:1-8

Hebrews 12:14-17

LESSON #15

ARE YOU READY TO MEET JESUS?

Text: Matthew 22:1-14
Key Verse: Vs. 14

Isaiah 64:6-7: Scarlet and crimson were two firm dyes that were hard to remove.

_____
_____
_____
_____
_____
_____
_____
_____

Romans 3:23
_____
_____
_____
_____
_____
_____
_____

Romans 6:23

_____
_____
_____
_____
_____
_____
_____

Isaiah 1:16-20

_____
_____
_____
_____
_____
_____
_____

Hebrews 9:27-28

_____
_____
_____
_____
_____
_____
_____

Luke 6:46

_____
_____
_____
_____
_____
_____
_____

Two Questions

1. Have you come to the place in your life that if you were to die today that you will go to Heaven? Why? (Hebrews 9:24)

_____
_____
_____
_____
_____
_____
_____

   a. Ephesians 6:1-13

_____
_____
_____
_____
_____
_____
_____

b. Luke 14:15-21

c. Romans 7:14-25

d. 2 Corinthians 5:10

2. Think about this scenario: You have passed from life to death and you're standing in the presence of God. He asks, "Why should II let you into Heaven?" what would your response be?

___

a. John 3:1-3

___

b. Isaiah 7:14

___

b. Matthew 1:18, 21, 23

___

c. John 1:12

___

d. Romans 10:9-10

___

Read the reference scriptures and share your understanding of the scripture in the space provided.

Judges 7:1-7

_____
_____
_____
_____
_____
_____
_____

2 Timothy 2:1-3

_____
_____
_____
_____
_____
_____
_____

a. Righteousness: Being and doing right (Isaiah 64:6)

_____
_____
_____
_____
_____
_____
_____

b. Shod: Shoes to protect the feet which will guide to the path of peace. (Psalms 119:105)

_____
_____
_____
_____
_____
_____
_____
_____
_____
_____

c. Faith: To trust in the ability of another. (Proverbs 3:5-6, Hebrews 11:6)

_____
_____
_____
_____
_____
_____
_____
_____
_____
_____
_____

d. Helmet: Protective head gear to protect the mind and thoughts (Romans 12:2)

e. Prayer: Spiritual communication, thanksgiving, adoration, and confession.

LESSON #16

STEPPING INTO TROUBLE

Text: John 5:1-8; Matthew 4:1-11

Trouble: To disturb the mental calm and contentment of; Something or someone that is a cause or source of disturbance, trials, tribulation, afflictions, misfortune.

_____
_____
_____
_____
_____

Three Elements of Trouble
1. Worry
2. Distress
3. Agitation

Read the reference scriptures and share your understanding of the scripture in the space provided.

Psalms 9:9

_____
_____
_____
_____
_____
_____

Psalms 31:7-9

Psalms 32:6-7

Psalms 41:1

Psalms 46:1

Psalms 54:6-7

Psalms 60:11

Psalms 66:13-14

Psalms 81:7

Psalms 91:15

Psalms 108:12

Psalms 138:7-8

Psalms 143:11-12

LESSON #17

SUBJECTIVE & INTERPERSONAL CONSEQUENCES

Text: Genesis 3:6-12, 15, 21; John 10:7-10

Key Verse: Vs.8-10

Subjective Consequences: Choices that we make that subjects us to shame, disrespect and dishonor of saved and unsaved people, which takes glory from God.

There are three elements to subjective consequences:

1. To hide or to avoid those whom we have violated. (Vs.10)
2. Avoid responsibility: to shift blame of our choices on someone or something else (vs.12)
3. Death: The spiritual disconnection or separation from God that cuts off communication because of sin. (vs.23-24)

Notes:

LESSON #18

RECOVERING FROM FAMILY CRISIS

Text: Ephesians 5:1-4; 15-17

Key Verse: Vs. 17

Paul's letter to the Church at Ephesus was one of his letters while in prison in Rome. Paul knew that the laws of man concerning husbands and wives violated the laws of God/Christ. The relationship between husband and wives had become violated by the husband not providing for his wife in all areas and the wife placing the children over her husband. (Mark 3:255, 27)

1. The one major problem (Ephesians 5:21; Luke 6:46)

_____
_____
_____
_____
_____
_____
_____
_____

2. Recovery process for wives (Ephesians 5:22-24)

_____
_____
_____
_____
_____
_____
_____

   a. **Submit:** Yield to, be subjected to.
   b. **Subject:** Under authority

3. Recovery process for husbands Ephesians 5:25-32)

_____
_____
_____
_____
_____
_____

   a. **Love:** a test of discipleship

4. **Recovery process for children (Ephesians 6:1-4)**

   a. **Obedience:** is a test of love
      i. **Children to parents, parents to God**
   b. **Provoke:** To nag or arbitrarily assert authority

5. **Provision for protection and blessing**
   a. **Wives: Submit**
   b. **Husbands: Love. Love will cause a wife to submit and children to obey**
   c. **Children: Obey**

Closing

Ephesians 6:10-13

LESSON #19

UNDERSTANDING THE SPIRITUAL AND PHYSICAL EFFECTS OF SIN

Text: Romans 6:1-23
Key Verse: vs.23

There are 6 Destructive Elements

1. **Sin darkens the mind**
   a. **Darken:** To be or become dark; without light

2. **Sin corrupts our feelings**
   a. **Corrupt:** bad, polluted, rotten

3. **Sin warps our will**
   a. **Warp:** To distort or cause to distort from the truth

4. **Sin redirects our affections**
   a. **Redirects**: To change the direction or focus.

5. **Sin blinds our eyes to the truth**
   a. **Blinds:** Unwilling or unable to perceive or understand.

6. **Sin sears our conscience**
   a. **Sears:** To make callous or unfeeling or harden.

Notes:

_____
_____
_____
_____
_____
_____
_____
_____
_____
_____

Part 2

HOW TO WALK CLOSE TO THE HEART OF GOD

INTRODUCTION: FIRST THINGS FIRST

Our prayer is that this lesson will minister to the whole man: mind, body, soul and spirit. Before starting this lesson read 2 Peter 1:1-10. Use the space provided below to share your reflections on the scripture passages.

Notes:

How to Walk Close to the Heart of God Study Lesson

Introduction: This lesson's purpose and goal is to give those who are in Christ Jesus the tools needed to develop in their lives the image and character of our Lord and Savior Jesus Christ.

Psalms 32:8

Joshua 1:8

There are four things needed in order to understand God's will:

1. Instruction
2. Wisdom
3. Knowledge
4. Understanding

Define each of the words in the space provided below.

Instruction

_____
_____
_____
_____
_____
_____
_____
_____
_____
_____

Wisdom

_____
_____
_____
_____
_____
_____
_____
_____
_____
_____

Knowledge

_____
_____
_____
_____
_____
_____
_____

Understanding

_____
_____
_____
_____
_____
_____
_____

Read Proverbs 4:1-7

According to Proverbs 4:1-7, which of the four words is the most powerful and why?

_____
_____
_____
_____
_____
_____

In order for us to walk close to God's heart we must first learn how to live holy. Holiness is the key ring that the other keys are attached to. It is the Lord's command that we live holy.

Read the reference scriptures and share your understanding of the scripture in the space provided.

Holiness

Psalms 99:1-9

_____
_____
_____
_____
_____
_____
_____
_____
_____

Leviticus 20:7

_____
_____
_____
_____
_____
_____
_____
_____
_____

Ephesians 1:3-4

Colossians 3:12

2 Timothy 1:7-9

1 Peter 1:15-16

_____
_____
_____
_____
_____
_____
_____

1 Peter 2:1-9

_____
_____
_____
_____
_____
_____
_____

Define each of the words in the space provided below.

Holiness

_____
_____
_____
_____
_____
_____

Holy

Hallowed

Consecrate

LESSON #1

DILIGENCE

Diligent: Giving persistent attention; persevering.

Persevering: To persist in anything taken. To maintain a purpose in spite of difficulty.

Diligence is an action demonstrated by what you do. To be willing to continue in the things of the Lord no matter what comes up against you to understand that nothing happens in our life without God's knowing and rewarding us whether good or evil.

Diligent people endure afflictions and only surrender to the will and the Word of God. God's works agrees only with His Word.

Read the reference scriptures and share your understanding of the scripture in the space provided.

1. Proverbs 4:23

_____
_____
_____
_____
_____
_____
_____

2. **Proverbs 21:5**

3. **Proverbs 22:28**

4. **Hebrews 6:10-11**

5. 2 Peter 1:4-10

6. 2 Peter 3:9-14

7. John 15:1-7

LESSON #2

VIRTUE

Virtue: Moral excellence, power

Moral: Pertaining to or concerned with the principles or rules of right conduct, or the distinction between right and wrong.

Excellence: Surpassing or knowing when and how to make the right choice.

Power: Might, strength and authority to make the right decision.

Virtue is faith in action. It is the power given by God through the Holy Spirit, that we may be able to endure all things that come upon us. To make the best of difficult or unsatisfactory situation. Knowing that if we abide in His Word, He will see us through. One thing I know for sure is that sin will take virtue right out of you.

Virtue will do 5 things;

1. Cause us sin;
2. Be honest;
3. To be just, right, or righteous;
4. To be pure, genuine, true, simple;
5. To be of good report or kind.

Read the reference scripture and share your understanding of the scripture in the space provided.

Virtue

1. Luke 6:17-19

   _____
   _____
   _____
   _____
   _____
   _____
   _____

2. Luke 8:41-46

   _____
   _____
   _____
   _____
   _____
   _____
   _____

3. Philippians 4:5-9

   _____
   _____
   _____
   _____
   _____
   _____
   _____

4. 1 Peter 2:9; 3:9

___

Power

5. Deuteronomy 8:18

___

6. Psalms 62:10-12

___

7. **Isaiah 40:25-26, 28-29**

8. **Acts 1:8**

9. **Acts 4:1-7**

10. 1 Corinthians 2:5; 4:20

11. 2 Timothy 1:1-7

12. 2 Peter 1:1-3

LESSON #3

KNOWLEDGE

Knowledge: The acquaintance with facts, truth, or principles as from study or investigation. Knowledge deals with the facts before a decision is made. Knowledge gives facts not opinions. It is the ability to understand, and apply information or instructions given to guide in all areas of life.

Read the reference scriptures and share your understanding of the scripture in the space provided.

1. 1 Kings 3:1-5

2. 2 Chronicles 1:1-12

3. Ecclesiastes 1:18

4. Proverbs 9:10

5. Hosea 4:1-6

6. Romans 10:1-3

_____
_____
_____
_____
_____
_____
_____
_____

7. Ephesians 1:17

_____
_____
_____
_____
_____
_____
_____
_____

8. 1 Timothy 2:1-6

_____
_____
_____
_____
_____
_____
_____

9. 2 Peter 3:18

_____
_____
_____
_____
_____
_____
_____
_____

Knowledge gives us the virtue and the power to stay diligent and to continue in holiness.

LESSON #4

TEMPERANCE

Temperance: self-control, the ability to resist evil or the ability to exercise self-control, moderation or self-restraint in action or statement.

Read the reference scriptures and share your understanding of the scripture in the space provided.

John 14:26

_____
_____
_____
_____
_____
_____

Acts 24:24-25

_____
_____
_____
_____
_____
_____
_____

Galatians 5:19-23

2 Peter 1; 16

LESSON #5

PATIENCE

Patience: Forbearance; endurance.

Forbearance: A refraining or holding back.

Endurance: To abide; to bear up under suffering.

Patience is the ability given by the Holy Spirit to forbear or refraining from action contrary to who you are. It is the ability to bear up under suffering.

Read the scriptures and share your understanding of the scripture in the space provided.

Matthew 18:23-31

_____
_____
_____
_____
_____
_____
_____
_____
_____
_____
_____

Romans 5:1-3; 15:1-6

2 Corinthians 6:1-4

2 Thessalonians 1:1-4

LESSON #6

GODLINESS

Godliness: To have the faith to believe that all takes place in my life, good or bad, as a believer in the Body of Christ, is somehow being used to mold my character to mirror that of my Father.

It involves living my life according God's will. This disciplined lifestyle builds quality and allows me to develop the seven character traits that will cause me to have a reverent fear of God's presence.

1. Knowledge: to know
2. Veneration: A feeling of awe, respect and reverence.
3. Affection: Feelings, passion (good or bad)
4. Dependence: The state of relying on or needing someone or something for aid or support.
5. Submission: To yield or to be subject to.
6. Gratitude: The quality of being grateful or thankful.
7. Obedience: To submit or obey.

Read the reference scriptures and share your understanding of the scripture in the space provided.

1. 1 Timothy 2:1-3,10

_____
_____
_____
_____
_____

2. 1 Timothy 3:16

___

3. 1 Timothy 4:7-8

___

4. Titus 1:1

___

5. 2 Peter 3:9-11

___

LESSON #7 & #8

BROTHERLY KINDNESS/BROTHERLY LOVE

Brotherly Kindness: To show grace or favor

Brotherly Love: To love one as if they are a brother; a love indicating the closest fellowship as of man to man.

Read the reference scriptures and share your understanding of the scripture in the space provided.

John 15:9, 12-13, 17

_____
_____
_____
_____
_____
_____
_____

Romans 12:9-10

_____
_____
_____
_____
_____
_____
_____

Romans 13:10

Galatians 5:13-14

1 Corinthians 13:1-8

1 Thessalonians 4:9

Hebrews 13:1

1 Peter 1:7

1 John 4:7-12; 16-21

Titus 2:1-8

Hebrews 12:1-3

James 5:10

Part 3

THE BLESSING, LOSS AND RESTORATION OF DOMINION

LESSON #1

THE BLESSING OF DOMINION

Day 1: Genesis 1:1-5
Day 2: Genesis 1:6-8

Firmament: The space that separates the clouds from the sea.

Day 3: Genesis 1:9-1 The separation of water from land.

Day 4: Lights in heaven; the rule of the sun and the moon over day and night.

Day 5-7: Genesis 1:20-23; The creation of all animals, fish, birds, man and a day of rest.

Genesis 2:1-5 God's review of His plan for man's dominion

Vs. 6 The first underground sprinkler system

Vs. 7-9 Provision for living

Preparation for His Son Adam's Wedding (Genesis 1:15-17, 19-20)

Wedding Ceremony for Adam (Genesis 1:21-25)

They enjoyed the glory and splendor of heaven and the beauty of life and comfort on earth. (Read Psalms 8:1-9)

God's counsel with the Son and the Holy Spirit. Vs 26-30

Check Your Understanding

1. In reading the account of Creation, what objects did God give dominion to?

   _____
   _____
   _____
   _____
   _____

2. Why does man have the right to govern or control?

   _____
   _____
   _____
   _____
   _____

3. Why does man have the indisputable and sovereign right of dominion?

   _____
   _____
   _____
   _____
   _____

Dominion: The power or right of governing and controlling, sovereign.

Sovereign: Supreme; preeminent, indisputable, sovereign right.

Preeminent: Above or before others, superior, surpassing.

Indisputable: Not disputable or deniable; uncontestable; unquestionable, real, valid.

Read: Genesis 3:1-24 The Cause of Man's Loss of Dominion. Share your understanding of the scripture in the space provided.

_____
_____
_____
_____
_____
_____
_____
_____
_____
_____
_____
_____
_____
_____
_____
_____
_____
_____
_____
_____
_____
_____
_____
_____
_____
_____

LESSON #2

THE LOSS OF DOMINION

Read: Genesis 3:1-5

Let's list the damages.

Subtle: Wise, crafty, wily, shrewd.

Beguiled: To be deceived, to delude.

Deceive: To mock, lead astray, to lie, oppress, entice.

The serpent enticed the woman and the woman enticed the man.

Delude: To mislead the mind or to deceive or fool.

Mock: To deride or jeer.

Deride: To laugh at or to turn up your nose at.

Three items of Lure (vs. #6)

1. She saw
2. It was pleasant
3. She desired it. (2 Samuel 11:1-3)

Saw: To perceive

Pleasant: To be desirable

Desire: To delight in or long for.

The Wedges in Their Dominion

(Vs. #7-8) They gain the knowledge of sin, evil, guilt, shame, blame, deceit, and lies.

> Vs. 9-12 The Call to Fellowship
> Vs. 13-15 God's plan to restore dominion
> Vs. 16-24 Judgment

Genesis Chapter 4: The Consequences of Sin

Key Verse: 26 The attempt to through Enosh to restore dominion

Genesis Chapter 6: The attempt to restore dominion through Noah

Throughout history the Lord attempted to use prophets, kings, and judges, to try to restore dominion, and every attempt failed because of man's sinful nature.

Notes:
_____
_____
_____
_____
_____
_____
_____
_____
_____
_____
_____
_____

LESSON #3

THE RESTORATION OF DOMINION

How to Recover Dominion

The Three Elements to Recovery

1. **Repentance (1John 1:9)**

   _____
   _____
   _____
   _____
   _____
   _____
   _____
   _____

2. **Reconciliation (2 Corinthians 5:17)**

   _____
   _____
   _____
   _____
   _____
   _____
   _____
   _____

3. **Restoration (Psalms 51:12)**

_____
_____
_____
_____
_____
_____
_____
_____
_____
_____

Repentance: To turn around or to make an about face.

Reconciliation: The bringing together of God and man a union of peace.

Restoration: To replace, refund.

Seven Steps to Reconciliation (Psalms 51:7-12)

_____
_____
_____
_____
_____
_____
_____
_____
_____
_____

Steps to Restoration (Ephesians 5:21 Both Husband and Wife)

Vs. 22-24 Wife

_____
_____
_____
_____
_____
_____
_____
_____
_____
_____

Submit: To yield or be subject to. **(Colossians 3:18)**

Vs. 25-31 Husband

_____
_____
_____
_____
_____
_____
_____
_____
_____
_____

Love is demonstrated by what you say and followed by actions. It is learned from God. (1 Corinthians 13:4-7)

Key Verse: Vs. #13

_____
_____
_____
_____
_____
_____
_____
_____
_____
_____
_____
_____
_____
_____
_____
_____
_____
_____
_____
_____
_____
_____
_____
_____

If follow these instructions it will cause us again to enjoy the splendor and glory of Creation and the blessings of God in the earth.

Part 4

FROM THE GARDEN TO THE CROSS

INTRODUCTION: ROOT CAUSE

Pt 4: From the Garden to the Cross deals with why the Lord destroyed the earth and mankind the first time as well as the events leading up to the expelling of Adam and Eve from the Garden. We will review the events that occurred during Adam's lifetime. For it was after he sinned that the world went into a tailspin that affected all of his descendents. Mankind became increasingly evil and eventually God destroyed them except for Noah and his family.

Time will not permit us to go through every step, but let's trap the main events. Come, let us see this thing unfold. Let's search the root cause of sin.

LESSON #1

WHERE IT ALL BEGAN

As we look in the book of Genesis, chapter 3, we find Adam and his wife hiding after they ate the fruit from the Tree of Knowledge of Good and Evil.

> *"And they heard the voice of the Lord God walking in the garden in the cool of the day: and Adam and his wife hid themselves from the presence of the Lord God amongst the <u>trees of the garden."</u> Genesis 3:8*

Sin became an infection that affected every generation of mankind from Adam to the present day. The first two children of Adam and Eve were Cain and Abel. The two sons were symbolic of Good and Evil, just like the Tree of Knowledge of Good and Evil in The Garden of Eden. The iniquity of Adam continued unfortunately with his oldest son, Cain. In a fit of jealousy, he killed his brother Abel and received the consequence of becoming a fugitive and having to work harder to farm the land that used to produce easily for him.

> *"And he said, What hast thou done? the voice of thy brother's blood crieth unto me from the ground. And now art thou cursed from the earth, which hath opened her mouth to receive thy brother's blood from thy hand; When thou tillest the ground, it shall not henceforth yield unto thee her strength; a fugitive and a vagabond shaly <u>thou be in the earth."</u> Genesis 4:10-12*

Why was Cain's sacrifice not accepted by the Lord?

_____
_____
_____
_____
_____
_____
_____
_____
_____

I believe the daughters of men spoken of in Genesis 6:2 were from Cain's lineal descent. After the death of Abel, the Bible says that Adam knew his wife and bare a son Seth. I believe that it is through the lineal descent of Enosh who was from Seth in Genesis 4:26, that says then begin men to call upon the name of the Lord. I believe that the sons of God in Genesis 6:2 are from Enoch.

Let's look at the genealogy of Adam through his son, Seth.

Adam was 130 when Seth was born; Seth was 105 when he had Enosh; Adam was then 235. Enosh was 90 when Cainan was born, Adams was then 325. Cainan was 70 when Mahalaleel was 65. When Jared was born, Adam was 460. Jared was 162 when Enoch was born, Adam was 622. Enoch was 65 when Methuselah was born, Adam was 687. Methuselah was 187 when Lamech was born, Adam was 874. And why do we remember Lamech? He was the father of Noah. Lamech was 56 when he was born and Adam died at 9:30. **(Genesis 5:3-23)**

³And Adam lived an hundred and thirty years, and begat a son in his own likeness, after his image; and named him Seth: ⁴After he begot Seth, the days of Adam were eight hundred years; and he had sons and daughters. ⁵So all the days that Adam lived were nine hundred and thirty years; and he died. ⁶Seth lived one hundred and five years, and begot Enosh. ⁷After he begot Enosh, Seth lived eight hundred and seven years, and had sons and daughters. ⁸So all the days of Seth were nine hundred and twelve years; and he died. ⁹Enosh lived ninety years, and begot [a]Cainan. ¹⁰After he begot Mahalalel, Cainan lived eight hundred forty years, and had sons and daughters. ¹¹So all the days of Cainan were nine hundred and ten years; and he died. ¹²Cainan lived seventy years, and begot Mahalalel. ¹³After he begot Mahalalel, Cainan lived eight hundred and forty years, and had sons and daughters. ¹⁴So all the days of Cainan were nine hundred and ten years; and he died.

¹⁵Mahalalel lived sixty-five years, and begot Jared. ¹⁶After he begot Jared, Mahalalel lived eight hundred and thirty years, and had sons and daughters.¹⁷So all the days of Mahalalel were eight hundred and ninety-five years; and he died. ¹⁸Jared lived one hundred and sixty-two years, and begot Enoch. ¹⁹After he begot Enoch, Jared lived eight hundred years, and had sons and daughters. ²⁰So all the days of Jared were nine hundred and sixty-two years; and he died. ²¹Enoch lived sixty-five years, and begot Methuselah. ²²After he begot Methuselah, Enoch walked with God three hundred years, and had sons and daughters. ²³So all the days of Enoch were three hundred and sixty-five years." Genesis 5:3-23

It is amazing to see that Adam witnessed the suffering of 8 generations as a direct result of his own sin. The full genealogy is found in **Genesis 5:1-32**

What other insights can you find in Genesis Chapter 5?

LESSON #2

GRACE FOUND IN AN UNEXPECTED PLACE

⁵Then the Lord saw that the wickedness of man was great in the earth, and that every intent of the thoughts of his heart was only evil continually. ⁶And the Lord was sorry that He had made man on the earth, and He was grieved in His heart. ⁷So the Lord said, "I will destroy man whom I have created from the face of the earth, both man and beast, creeping thing and birds of the air, for I am sorry that I have made them." <u>⁸But Noah found grace in the eyes of the Lord." Genesis 6:5-8</u>

Noah was symbolic of a type of Christ, and it was through him that man was spared by the grace of God. This was the beginning of the First Covenant that God made with man. In **Genesis 9:12-16**, God lays out His covenant.

"And God said: "This is the sign of the covenant which I make of the covenant which I make between Me and you, and every living creature that is with you, for perpetual generations: ¹³I set My rainbow in the cloud, and it shall be for the sign of the covenant between Me and the earth. ¹⁴It shall be, when I bring a cloud over the earth, that the rainbow shall be seen in the cloud; ¹⁵and I will remember My covenant which is between Me and you and every living creature of all flesh; the waters shall never again become a flood to destroy all flesh. ¹⁶The rainbow shall be in the cloud, and I will look on it to remember the everlasting covenant between God and every living creature of all flesh that is on the earth." ¹⁷And God said to Noah, "This is the sign of the covenant which I have established between Me and all the flesh that is on the earth." **Genesis 9:12-16**

It was during The Flood that the remaining generations of Adam were destroyed from off the face of the earth, with the exception of Noah and his family. The Ark rested in the seventh month, on the seventeenth day of the month, upon the mountains of Ararat. **(Genesis 8:4)** After the flood waters subsided, Noah built an altar and offered a burnt offering which is a form of worship.

And the Lord smelled a soothing aroma. Then the Lord said in His heart, "I wil never again curse the ground for man's sake, although the imagination of man's heart is evil from his youth; nor will I again destroy every living things as I have done. 22 "While the earth remains, seedtime and harvest, cold and heat, winter and summer, and day and night shall not cease." Genesis 8:21-22

The families became settled after The Flood and the sin nature of Adam resurfaces through Noah. He plants a vineyard and gets drunk and thereby curses his grandson Canaan, one of the son's of Ham. **(Genesis 9:20-25)** The history of Noah's sons can be found in **Genesis Chapters 10 & 11.**

How did Noah curse his grandson by becoming drunk?

_____
_____
_____
_____
_____
_____

Throughout the history of man, the Lord has always extended His grace. Every prophet, priest and king in the Old Testament were symbolic of a type of Christ. The various sacrifices of sheep, goats, pigeons and doves were all symbolic of the shed blood of Jesus. These sacrifices were required until the Lord decided that the blood of bulls and goats would not satisfy the sin debt.

"But Christ came as High Priest of the good things to come, with the greater and more perfect tabernacle not made with hands, that is, not of this creation. 12 Not with the blood of goats and calves, but with His own blood He entered the Most Holy Place once for all, having obtained eternal redemption. 13 For if the blood of buls and goats and the ashes of a heifer, sprinkling the unclean, sanctifies for the purifying of the flesh, 14 how much more shall the blood of Christ, who through the eternal Spirit offered Himself without spot to God, cleanse your conscience fromdead works to serve the living God?" Hebrews 9:11-14

In your studies of Abraham, Isaac, Jacob and Moses, you will find that God made them al a promise that they would become a great nation. These promises were made while the people of God were in captivity.

Locate the scriptures where God makes Promises to His Patriarchs.

Abraham:

_____
_____
_____
_____

Isaac:

Jacob:

Moses:

What are your thoughts on promises and captivity? How can this be applied to your life?

LESSON #3

REVIEWING THE CROSS & REEVALUATING CHRISTIANITY

"Now there arose a new king over Egypt, who did not know Joseph ⁹And he said to his peopl, "Look, the people of the children of Israel are more and mightier than we;" **Genesis 1:8-9**

This multitude is symbolic of the Church of Jesus Christ, so this brings us to the events leading up to the cross. Jesus outlines the starting events of the signs of His return in **Matthew 24:1-35**

_____
_____
_____
_____
_____
_____
_____

"As it was in the days of Noah so it is in our time. But as the days of Noah were, so also will the coming of the Son of Man be. ³⁸For as in the days before the flood, they were eating and drinking marrying and giving in marriage, until the day that Noah entered the ark," **Matthew 24:37-38**

Also in **2Timothy 3:1-5**

But know this, that in the last days [a]perilous times will come: ²For men will be lovers of themselves, lovers of money, boasters, proud, blasphemers, disobedient to parents, unthankful, unholy, ³unloving, [b]unforgiving, slanderers, without self-control, brutal, despisers of good, ⁴traitors, headstrong, haughty, overs of pleasure rather than lovers of God, ⁵having a form of godliness but denying its power. And from such people turn away!" 2 Timothy 3:1-6

Deception #1: Denominationalism

It is man's misuse of scripture that has deceived the Church of Jesus Christ. The first deception of the Church is Denominationalism. Your proclamation of Being Baptist, Holiness, Church of God in Christ, Pentecostal, Jesus Only, Methodist, Evangelical, or any other denomination has absolutely nothing to do with salvation.

"He said to them, "But who do you say that I am?" ¹⁶ Simon Peter answered and said, "You are the Christ, the Son of the living God." ¹⁷ Jesus answered and said to him, "Blessed are you, Simon Bar-Jonah, for flesh and blood has not revealed this to you, but My Father who is in heaven. ¹⁸ And I also say to you that you are Peter, and on this rock I will build My church, and the gates of Hades shall not [g] prevail against it. ¹⁹ And I will give you the keys of the kingdom of heaven, and whatever you bind on earth [h] will be bound in heaven, and whatever you loose on earth will be loosed in heaven." Matthew 16:15-19

On Peter's profession of faith, Jesus did not say upon this Baptis rock or upon this Pentecostal rock, I will build my church. It is this denominational sickness that we have imposed on the Church of Jesus Christ that has crippled the people of God. Denominationalism has served as a platform for men and women who claim to be called pastors and ministers of the Gospel, who use it for their own greed and gain. Denominationalism is used to divide the Church of Jesus Christ and because of this the Church has lost its power in the community. Any man or woman who uses this device is an enemy of the cross of Christ. The Church of Jesus Churst is built completely upon faith in the fact that Jesus was born of the virgin birth and was sent into the world to die for the sins of man.

Isaiah 7:14 shares the prophecy of Christ's coming, it says, **"therefore the Lord Himself shall give you a sign; behold a virgin shall conceive, and bear a son, and shall call his name Immanuel."** And it is fulfilled in **Matthew 1:23**, which says, **"Behold a virgin shall be with child, and shall bring forth a son and they shall call his name Emmanuel which being interpreted is God with us."**

> "And she will bring forth a Son, and you shall call His name Jesus, for He will save His people from their sins." Matthew 1:21

It is through this virgin birth that Jesus came into the world to be the Savior of the world, to be the Savior of mankind. It is His life that can be found in all four gospels that gives us a picture of what our relationship with God should be like **Isaiah 53:1-12** describes the brutal crucifixion and it is in three of the gospels where you can find it fulfilled.

Our salvation is based on these elements:

- **Do you believe that He died on that shameful cross which is an emblem of misery and shame for your sins?**

- **Do you believe that He rose the third day according to the scripture? 1 Corinthians 15:1-4**

The reason for this salvation is because we were all born through the fallen nature of Adam which made all of us sinners.

Romans 3:23 For all have sinned and come short of the Glory of God, but our salvation comes through Jesus Christ our Lord. This salvation was at a great cost, one that o ordinary man could pay and the cost was the cross. It is through this cost that everyone that confesses Christ are transitioned from sinners to saints.

What is a sinner? One who falls short, a rebellious wicked person.

This was all of us because of the fall of Adam. It is because of this fallen nature that we will often find ourselves in the valley of decision.

What is the valley of decision? It is where you will find a person whose life is full of trouble and turmoil. They are at the place of making a decision.

Proverbs 14:25

_____
_____
_____
_____
_____
_____

When sickness has brought you to the very edge of death, you are at the valley of decision. Every situation in your life will bring you to the valley of decision. Isaiah1:18

What is the valley? It is any place period or situation that is filled with fear, gloom, and despair.

Decision: the act of need for making up one's mind.

"Now therefore, fear the LORD, serve Him in sincerity and in truth and put away the gods which your fathers served on the other side of the River and in Egypt. Serve the LORD!15 And if it seems evil to you to serve the LORD, choose for yourselves this day whom you will serve, whether the gods which your father served that were on the other side of the River, or the gods of the Amorites, in whose land you dwell. But as for me and my house, we will serve the LORD." Joshua 24:14-15

It is in the valley of decision where you will decide which road to stay on. The three roads in question are Jericho, Damascus and Emmaus. These three roads in scripture are symbolic of our lives Jericho is the road that all of us are born on, not by choice but because of our sin nature.

Psalms 51:5 says, "Behold, I was shapen in iniquity and in sin did my mother conceive me." It is on this road where the enemy seeks to take our lives.

"The thief does not come except to steal, and to kill, and to destroy. I have come that they may have life, and that they may have it more abundantly." John 10:10

The road to Jericho is found in **Luke 10:25-37**. The items of destruction on this road are found in **Galatians 5:19-21**. The next road is the road to Damascus, it is the road of decision where you will meet Jesus. When the course of life has caused great difficulty and we begin to look for a different way, it is on Damascus Road where there is opportunity for the new birth to take place.

What are the items of destruction that are found in Galatians 5:19-21?

_____
_____
_____
_____
_____
_____

Acts 9:1-6, Key verse 6 where Paul asks a question, **"And he trembling and astonished said, What will thou have me to do? And the Lord said unto him, Arise, and go into the city, and it shall be told thee what thou must do."**

It is on Damascus Road where Paul met Jesus. It is on Damascus Road where **John 3:16** comes to life. **"For God so loved the world that he gave his only begotten son that whosoever believeth in him should not perish but have everlasting life."** Who are the whosevers? The murderers, thieves, the drunks, the drug user and the dealer, the prostitute, the fornicator, the adulterer, and anything else not listed. It is on Damascus where these scriptures come to life.

Matthew 11:28 says, "Come unto me all ye that labor and are heavy laden and I will give you rest." and again in **John 14:6, Jesus says unto him," I am the way, the truth, and the life: no man cometh to the Father but by Me."**

Then there is Emmaus Road where we follow Jesus until His return. It is a road of every day growth with a rewarding end.

Luke 24:13-30.

_____
_____
_____
_____
_____
_____
_____
_____

Deception #2: The Ornamental Cross

The second deception of the Church is the pretty picture of the cross that hangs in and on the outside of our buildings. Let's really look at the cross. In our time, the cross has taken on the form of a piece of jewelry or an attractive ornament for a Christmas tree, even as a fashion statement among believers.

Let's see how Jesus viewed it. Read Matthew 26:36-39.

_____
_____
_____
_____
_____
_____
_____
_____

The cross was a means of the cruelest of deaths for our Lord and Savior Jesus Christ. Read Mark 15:29-34, 37.

___

The cross was meant for murderers and slaves but this was the choice of God our Father for our salvation.

The cross dismantles the ceremonies and sacrifices of the Old Testament. Read Hebrews 10:1-10.

___

Now my question to you is, are you willing to bare a cross for Jesus?

Matthew 16:21-24

Our cross symbolizes the burdens of life; severe affliction or trials that come because of our obedience to the Word of God with faith, self-denial, daily dying to self, to fulfill the will of the Lord and dying to sin daily. It is because of these deceptions that the church has been taken under siege.

What does it mean to be taken under siege? To capture to be made subject to or to be in subjection or submission, to be taken advantage of by any person, place or thing other than the Holy Spirit.

Matthew 11:12

_____
_____
_____
_____
_____
_____

Malachi 3:8-10. The purpose is to bring a person to the point of guilt and thereby control them.

Before going any further, read **Leviticus 27:1-19, key verse 13, 15 and 19.**

_____
_____
_____
_____
_____
_____

Deception #3 Tithing

Another deception is the false teaching on tithes and offering. It is what wicked men do not want you to know. The famous passage of scripture for tithes and offering is Malachi wrote to Israel about their negligence in their tithing, not to bring guilt to them but to remind them of their agreement with the Lord. If we are going to go by the Old Testament than we need to teach it all. For example, if a person is tithing ten percent of his or earnings, then the scripture says that he can redeem five percent of what the values is that he has given an upon returning that was taken, add five percent. Why is this not being taught?

Do you understand how to honor the Lord in your giving? How is this reflected in your sacrificial giving at your local church?
_____
_____
_____
_____
_____

Deception #4: Speaking in Tongues

The next deception is speaking in tongue as evidence of the Holy Spirit. This is not true.

John 14:26
_____
_____
_____
_____
_____

Acts 1:8

Ephesians 1:12-14

Deception #5 Manmade Holidays

The most powerful of all the deceptions are these manmade holidays. Nowhere in scripture will you find that Jesus was born on that pagan holiday that we call Christmas. It is an abomination to the Lord to include His birth with pagan worship.

Jeremiah 10:1-18

Another example is Easter. We have equated Passover and Pentecost with the pagan holiday Easter, and have renamed it Resurrection Sunday. We have also taught our children that Easter Egg hunts are a part of the Resurrection and with our children Santa Claus us more popular than Jesus.

Jeremiah 23:1-4

_____
_____
_____
_____
_____
_____
_____
_____
_____
_____

2 Corinthians 5:17

_____
_____
_____
_____
_____
_____
_____
_____
_____
_____

Notes:

FINAL WORDS FROM THE AUTHOR

What do we mean when we day new? It means to start over. This is a new season for those who are in Christ Jesus; meaning it is suitable, proper fitting or right time. It's time to renew your covenant with the Lord.

Joshua 24:14-26

_____
_____
_____
_____
_____
_____
_____

John 15:1-12

_____
_____
_____
_____
_____
_____
_____

May the Grace of God keep you as we go through these difficult times. My desire is that this book will encourage the believer, draw a pitcher of salvation to the sinner, and restore the backslider.

ABOUT THE AUTHOR

Charles E. Young, Sr. was born in Highland Park, Michigan. He is the fourth oldest son of eleven children. At the age of 12, he experienced the weather phenomena of it raining on one side of the street while the sun shone on the side where he stood. This opened his eyes to the reality of God, although it would be six more years before he'd surrender his life to the Lordship of Jesus Christ. Charles survived the 67' Riots in Detroit and later joined the US Navy in 1972. He proudly served his country during the Vietnam War and was discharged in 1974. He answered the call to ministry a few years later in 1979 and has served God's people ever since.

He furthered his education by receiving a BA of Theology from the Detroit School of Ministry in 2001. On March 23rd, 2003, Rev Young was called to pastor and under the guidance of the Holy Spirit, he founded First Resurrection Evangelical Ministries which is currently his home. Pastor loves teaching and preaching, his debut book comes from the many lessons that he has taught at First Resurrection and they stem from his and the member's personal life experiences. The most powerful lesson to him was the clear understanding of the Cross.

Printed in the USA
CPSIA information can be obtained
at www.ICGtesting.com
LVHW041111160524
780223LV00001B/62